D1413898

Drums

A Level One Reader

By Cynthia Klingel and Robert B. Noyed

The
Child's
World®

Bang, bang. Rat-a-tat. It is time to play the drums!

People all over the world play drums.

4

People play drums to make music.

People play drums to create a beat.

You can make many
sounds on a drum.

You can use drumsticks
to hit the drums.

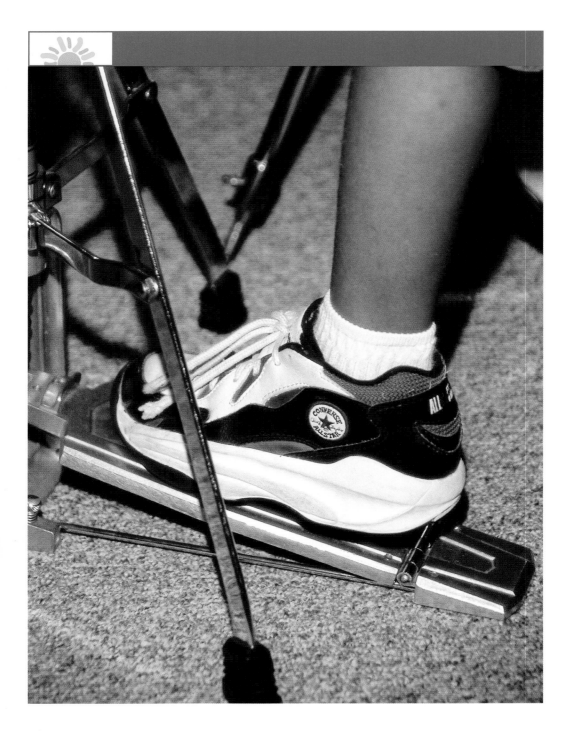

14

People also use their feet to make sounds from drums.

There are many kinds
of drums.

Some drums are big.
Some are small.

Bang, bang. Rat-a-tat. It is fun to play the drums!

Word List

beat

create

drumsticks

sounds

Note to Parents and Educators

Welcome to Wonder Books®! These books provide text at three different levels for beginning readers to practice and strengthen their reading skills. Additionally, the use of nonfiction text provides readers the valuable opportunity to *read to learn*, not just to learn to read.

These leveled readers allow children to choose books at their level of reading confidence and performance. Nonfiction Level One books offer beginning readers simple language, word choice, and sentence structure as well as a word list. Nonfiction Level Two books feature slightly more difficult vocabulary, longer sentences, and longer total text. In the back of each Nonfiction Level Two book are an index and a list of books and Web sites for finding out more information. Nonfiction Level Three books continue to extend word choice and length of text. In the back of each Nonfiction Level Three book are a glossary, an index, and a list of books and Web sites for further research.

State and national standards in reading and language arts emphasize using nonfiction at all levels of reading development. Wonder Books® fill the historical void in nonfiction material for the primary grade readers with the additional benefit of a leveled text.

About the Authors

Cynthia Klingel has worked as a high school English teacher and an elementary school teacher. She is currently the curriculum director for a Minnesota school district. Cynthia Klingel lives with her family in Mankato, Minnesota.

Robert B. Noyed started his career as a newspaper reporter. Since then, he has worked in school communications and public relations at the state and national level. Robert B. Noyed lives with his family in Brooklyn Center, Minnesota.

Published by The Child's World®, Inc.
PO Box 326
Chanhassen, MN 55317-0326
800-599-READ
www.childsworld.com

Photo Credits
© Andre Jenny/Unicorn Stock Photos: cover
© 2003 David E. Myers/Stone: 5
© Joel Dexter/Unicorn Stock Photos: 13
© 2003 Keren Su/Stone: 21
© Mark Richards/PhotoEdit: 18
© 2003 Randy Wells/Stone: 6
© Robert Brenner/PhotoEdit: 17
© Romie Flanagan: 2, 14
© Rudi Von Briel/PhotoEdit: 9
© Spencer Grant/PhotoEdit: 10

Project Coordination: Editorial Directions, Inc.
Photo Research: Alice K. Flanagan

Library of Congress Cataloging-in-Publication Data
Klingel, Cynthia Fitterer.
Drums / by Cynthia Klingel and Robert B. Noyed.
    p. cm. — (An Easy reader)
"Wonder books leveled readers"—P. 23.
ISBN 1-56766-946-8 (lib. bdg. : alk. paper)
1. Drum—Juvenile literature. [1. Drum.]
I. Noyed, Robert B. II. Title. III. Series.
ML1035 .K55 2001
786.9—dc21
                    00-011368

24